Millie & Kuku's Great Discovery

Bruce Khumalo

Millie the millipede

stood **admiring** herself in the **simmering** savannah **sun**.

Her **body** stood out against **the sand,** **shining** beautifully, **black as coal**.

Underneath her body were

legs,
    legs
        and
            more legs

– **so many legs** she looked
like a train on stilts.

She sang out loud:

'Birds have **two legs**,
cats have **four**.

Insects have **six legs**
and what is **more**,

spiders have **eight**,
but **who** in the world
knows my **trait**?

Is it in my **name**?
Who knows how many
legs a **millipede** has?

The total number is
truly great!'

Leo the leopard heard Millie's song and said:

'I have **so many spots** no animal can count.

I am the **top cat** for spots on a coat.

I can **count** all my legs – **1, 2, 3, 4.**

But, **Millie**,
counting your legs is truly
not
my
sport.'

Millie walked on and
continued to sing:

'Birds have **two legs**,
cats have **four**.

Insects have **six legs**
and what is **more**,

spiders have **eight**,
but **who** in the world
knows my **trait**?

Is it in my **name**?
Who knows how many legs
a **millipede** has?

The total number is
truly great!'

Zeb the zebra

was grazing nearby when
he heard Millie's tune
and said:

'My coat has **so many stripes** that I must say I don't know the **colour** of my own **skin**.

Am I **white** with **black** stripes

or am I **black** with **white** stripes?

What really is the **answer** to that **riddle**?

I can **count** the **number** of my **legs** without getting into a **muddle** – 1, 2, 3, 4 and **that is my lot**.

But counting the number of your legs, Millie, is truly **not my sport.**'

Millie felt special and
walked on, singing her song:

'Birds have **two legs**,
cats have **four**.

Insects have **six legs**
and what is **more**,

spiders have **eight**,
but **who** in the world
knows my **trait**?

Is it in my **name**?
Who knows how many legs
a **millipede** has?

The total number is
truly great!'

Kuku the hen

heard Millie's song and gave a **wide smile**, for this was her **sport**.

'My **eyes** are my **prize**,
so I'm **hard** to **surprise**.

I can **solve** your problem
if you give me a **chance**.

I can see from **different
angles** in only one glance.

I can count my legs –
1, 2 and I'm through.

Now let me try and count
all of yours too.'

She **stretched out** on the rocks the bright morning sun had warmed and **began counting** right away.

'**Go ahead, Kuku**. I'm sure you'll agree when you see that counting up

all my legs

is **too great a task** for you,' said Millie.

Kuku **didn't listen** to Millie and started counting.

She counted **all morning**. She really used her head.

She was **still counting** past noon, when the sun was in **full bloom**.

Millie was sure Kuku would **give up soon**.

But she was **still counting** as the evening sun turned **red**.

Suddenly Kuku shouted:

'It's 750! It's 750! It's not 1,000!
I've done it – I've got it!

The number of your legs is **not 1,000**.'

Millie jumped up and curled into **a tight ball.**

But **Millie** knew all the animals would **hear** about **Kuku's** counting and believe **she'd got it right**.

So **today**, if you come across a millipede and **touch it**, it will **curl up into a ball** to **defend** its **name**.

Just in case you can
also **count its legs**
and prove
Kuku was right.

*To Tyrone, Bethany, Paige, Noah,
Zachary – my biggest little fans.*

*And the most beautiful part of my life;
the reason I can be all that I am.
My wife Shelly.*

I love and cherish you all dearly.

First published in 2021

Text © Bruce Khumalo

Images © Fuad Sy

Printed in Great Britain
by Amazon

84210189R10018